Dear Parent:

Congratulations! Your child is taking the first steps on an exciting journey. The destination? Independent reading!

STEP INTO READING® will help your child get there. The program offers books at five levels that accompany children from their first attempts at reading to reading success. Each step includes fun stories, fiction and nonfiction, and colorful art. There are also Step into Reading Sticker Books, Step into Reading Math Readers, and Step into Reading Phonics Readers— a complete literacy program with something to interest every child.

Learning to Read, Step by Step!

Ready to Read   Preschool–Kindergarten
• big type and easy words • rhyme and rhythm • picture clues
For children who know the alphabet and are eager to begin reading.

Reading with Help   Preschool–Grade 1
• basic vocabulary • short sentences • simple stories
For children who recognize familiar words and sound out new words with help.

Reading on Your Own   Grades 1–3
• engaging characters • easy-to-follow plots • popular topics
For children who are ready to read on their own.

Reading Paragraphs   Grades 2–3
• challenging vocabulary • short paragraphs • exciting stories
For newly independent readers who read simple sentences with confidence.

Ready for Chapters   Grades 2–4
• chapters • longer paragraphs • full-color art
For children who want to take the plunge into chapter books but still like colorful pictures.

STEP INTO READING® is designed to give every child a successful reading experience. The grade levels are only guides. Children can progress through the steps at their own speed, developing confidence in their reading, no matter what their grade.

Remember, a lifetime love of reading starts with a single step!

For my son Calvin—
the original Quack
—M.A.

Text copyright © 1996 by Marsha Arnold. Illustrations copyright © 1996 by Lisa McCue.
All rights reserved under International and Pan-American Copyright Conventions. Published
in the United States by Random House Children's Books, a division of Random House, Inc.,
New York, and simultaneously in Canada by Random House of Canada Limited, Toronto.

www.stepintoreading.com

Educators and librarians, for a variety of teaching tools, visit us at
www.randomhouse.com/teachers

Library of Congress Cataloging-in-Publication Data
Arnold, Marsha Diane.
Quick, Quack, quick! / by Marsha Arnold ; illustrated by Lisa McCue.
    p.   cm. — (Step into reading. A step 2 book.)
SUMMARY: A very slow duckling saves his family during a crisis.
ISBN 0-679-87243-4 (trade) — ISBN 0-679-97243-9 (lib. bdg.)
[1. Ducks—Fiction. 2. Speed—Fiction.]   I. McCue, Lisa, ill. II. Title.
III. Series: Step into reading. Step 2 book.
PZ7.A7363 Qu 2003   [E]—dc21   2002013647

Printed in the United States of America   25 24 23 22 21 20 19 18 17 16

STEP INTO READING, RANDOM HOUSE, and the Random House colophon are registered
trademarks of Random House, Inc.

Quick, Quack, Quick!

by Marsha Arnold

illustrated by Lisa McCue

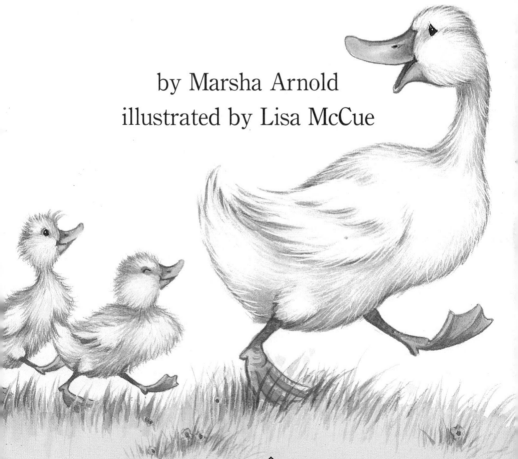

Random House New York

Into the barnyard
came a duck
and her ducklings.

All but one.

He stopped

to visit the baby pigs.

"Quick, Quack, quick!"
his mama called.

Quack started to follow.

Then he saw a butterfly.

"Quick, Quack, quick!"
his mama called.
"Quick, or the chickens
will eat all the corn."

Quack pecked
at a kernel of corn.
Then he heard the birds.

"Quick, Quack, quick!"
his mama called.
"To the pond.
It's time to swim."

Quack ate berries
along the path
to the pond.

"Quick, Quack, quick!"
his mama called.
"Into the water."

But instead
Quack played games
around a hollow log.
He danced on the log.
He hid in the log.

"Peep, peep,"

Quack said into the log.

"QUACK! QUACK!"

came out the other end.

Finally Quack jumped
into the water.

"Tails up,"
said his mama.

As the ducklings swam,
the sky changed
from blue to pink.

It was time to go home.
"Quick, Quack, quick!"
his mama called.

"Back to the barnyard.
Soon it will be dark
and Cat will go hunting."

Quack started to follow.
Then he saw
more berries.

One berry.

Two.

Three berries.

Four.

"Quick, Quack, quick!"
his mama called
from far away.
Quack had to stand
on top of the hollow log
to see his family.

But what was that behind them?

"Mama, Mama, look out!"
Quack called.
But she was
too far away to hear.

Quack jumped
off the log.
"Peep! Peep!" he said
into the log.

Quack's mama
heard a loud
QUACK! QUACK!
She turned around
and saw Cat!

Mama Duck
snapped her beak
and charged at Cat.

Cat ran away,
far, far away.
Quack's family
was saved!

"Dearest Quack,"
his mama said,
"for once I am glad
you were <u>not</u> quick!"